squid

spotted drum

parrot fish

fairy
basslets

squirrelfish

damselfish

cleaner
shrimp

nurse shark

trumpet fish

crab

APPLEGATE
LIBRARY

Presented by

Friends of the
Library

Octopus Alone

by Divya Srinivasan

VIKING

Octopus lay hidden in her cozy cave, enjoying the scene outside. Turtle chased squid, squid chased shrimp, and the puffer was getting nervous with all the chasing going on.

Then Octopus saw the seahorses bobbing along outside.

One little one peeked in.

Then another.

And another.

The seahorses found Octopus fascinating,
but she was shy and did not like to be noticed.

She tried to shoo them away.

But they thought she was playing, so they played too.

"I give up," Octopus sighed.

Squeezing out of her cave, she crawled
into the garden.

She changed colors just like that, and disappeared.
The seahorses swam away, wondering where she'd gone.

Sea snakes slithered in and out of holes.

Among the swaying anemones, baby dominos played hide-and-seek, while clownfish chased butterflies.

Tiny fish ate algae from a big fish's scales, leaving them sparkling clean.

Octopus was about to pounce on a juicy lobster, when she saw the little seahorses coming her way.

She went perfectly still. The lucky lobster slid into a crevice.

When the seahorses weren't disturbing her, they were delightful to watch. They wiggled and twirled, and one even did somersaults. It looked like so much fun!

It was hard for Octopus to keep still, but she did, and the merry seahorses moved on.

Octopus crept over to a thicket of stars. Jellyfish drifted past and headed beyond the reef.

"Where do they go?" She gazed at the shimmering shapes.

Suddenly she had a funny feeling.

The seahorses were staring.
For how long, she wondered!

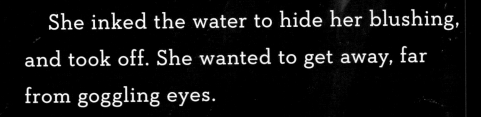

She inked the water to hide her blushing,
and took off. She wanted to get away, far
from goggling eyes.

After a while, she spied something interesting. A box full of delicious crabs!

Octopus squished herself into the cage . . .

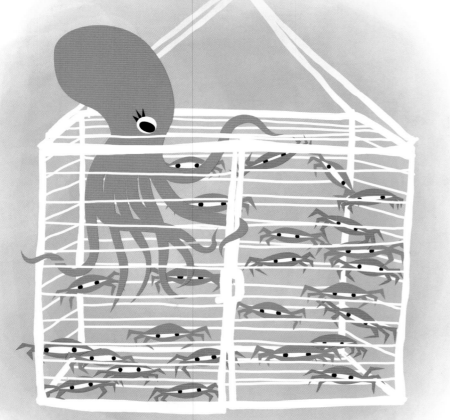

but the crabs began pinching.

She fiddled with the door, and it
opened. Out tumbled the frantic crabs.

Octopus was about to grab a few, when
she had *another* funny feeling.

A hungry eel was about to strike!

Octopus squirted a cloud of ink and swam

and swam

and swam.

When she finally stopped, she was far beyond the reef. Here the water was gloriously empty . . . no one watching, no one to hide from.

Whale song rose faintly from the deep. Octopus remembered the dancing seahorses.

She wiggled!

She twirled!

She even did a somersault!

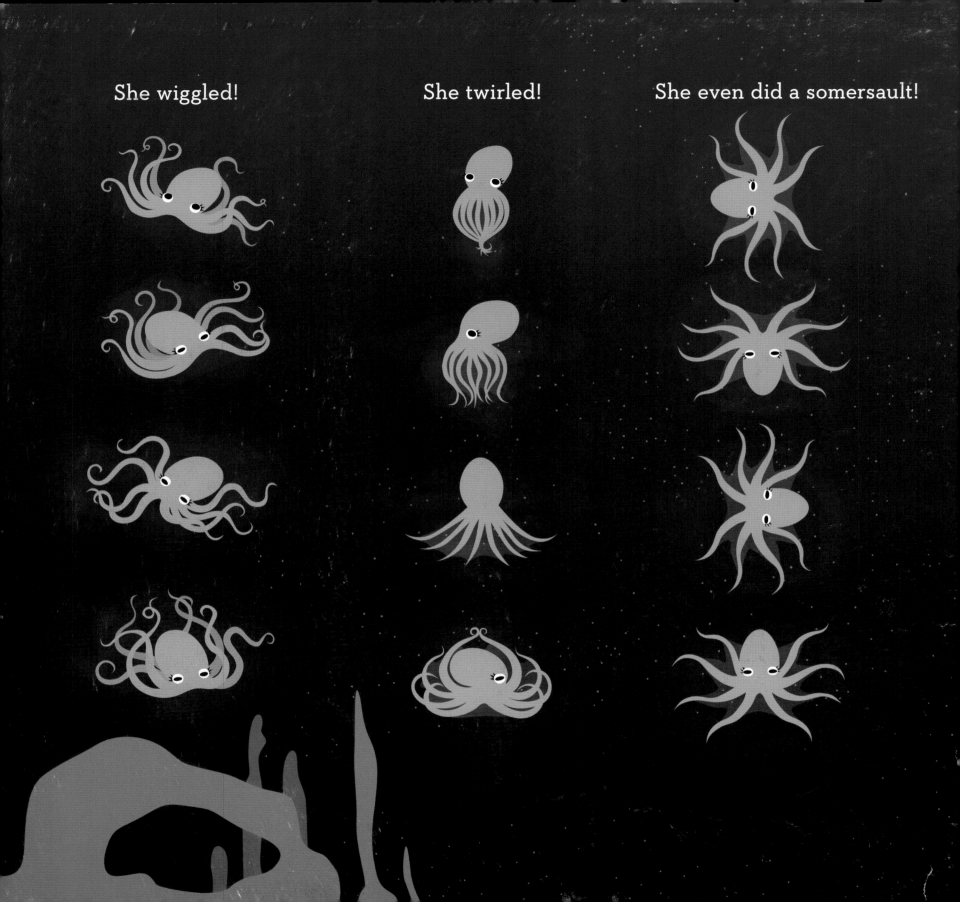

She was *so* happy to be alone.

Then she felt a rumbling in the waters below.

Whoosh!

A whale surged past, up and out of the water.

The whale crashed back down, leaving
a magnificent storm of bubbles.

The whale song faded into the distance
until all was quiet. Exhausted, Octopus fell asleep.

When Octopus awoke, she went outside. A lone
jellyfish drifted by. No one was around to disturb her
in this wonderful, quiet place.

But, after some time, she began thinking about the lively
reef, with its graceful anemones and slinking sea snakes.

Most of all, she wondered
what the seahorses were up to.

"I'd better go home and find out," she said, hurrying along.

When Octopus reached the reef, one little seahorse welcomed her home.

Then another.

And another.

Octopus was glad to be back with her friends.

For my friends.
I love you guys.
—Divya

VIKING

Published by the Penguin Group

Penguin Young Readers Group, 345 Hudson Street, New York, New York 10014, U.S.A.

Penguin Group (Canada), 90 Eglinton Avenue East, Suite 700, Toronto, Ontario, Canada M4P 2Y3 (a division of Pearson Penguin Canada Inc.)

Penguin Books Ltd, 80 Strand, London WC2R 0RL, England

Penguin Ireland, 25 St Stephen's Green, Dublin 2, Ireland (a division of Penguin Books Ltd)

Penguin Group (Australia), 250 Camberwell Road, Camberwell, Victoria 3124, Australia (a division of Pearson Australia Group Pty Ltd)

Penguin Books India Pvt Ltd, 11 Community Centre, Panchsheel Park, New Delhi - 110 017, India

Penguin Group (NZ), 67 Apollo Drive, Rosedale, Auckland 0632, New Zealand (a division of Pearson New Zealand Ltd.)

Penguin Books (South Africa) (Pty) Ltd, 24 Sturdee Avenue, Rosebank, Johannesburg 2196, South Africa

Penguin Books Ltd, Registered Offices: 80 Strand, London WC2R 0RL, England

First published in the United States of America by Viking, a division of Penguin Young Readers Group, 2013

10 9 8 7 6 5 4 3 2 1

Copyright © Divya Srinivasan, 2013

All rights reserved

LIBRARY OF CONGRESS CATALOGING-IN-PUBLICATION DATA

Srinivasan, Divya.

Octopus alone / by Divya Srinivasan.

p. cm.

Summary: Octopus leaves her cave in a lively reef because she is shy and the seahorses there find her fascinating, but when she finds a quieter, more peaceful spot she misses her home and friends.

ISBN 978-0-670-78515-5 (hardcover)

[1. Octopus—Fiction. 2. Marine animals—Fiction. 3. Bashfulness—Fiction.] I. Title.

PZ7.S77414Oct 2013   [E]—dc23   2012029678

Manufactured in China   Set in Neutraface Slab Text   Book design by Nancy Brennan

featherduster worms

nautilus

puffer fish

nudibranch

sea stars

topshell

butterfly fish

clownfish

domino damselfish

tube sponges

anemones

lobster

garden eels

sea urchins